Millions of Americans remember Dick and Jane (and Sally and Spot too!). The little stories with their simple vocabulary words and warmly rendered illustrations were a hallmark of American education in the 1950s and 1960s.

But the first Dick and Jane stories actually appeared much earlier—in the Scott Foresman Elson Basic Reader Pre-Primer, copyright 1930. These books featured short, upbeat, and highly readable stories for children. The pages were filled with colorful characters and large, easy-to-read Century Schoolbook typeface. There were fun adventures around every corner of Dick and Jane's world.

Generations of American children learned to read with Dick and Jane, and many still cherish the memory of reading the simple stories on their own. Today, Pearson Scott Foresman remains committed to helping all children learn to read—and love to read. As part of Pearson Education, the world's largest educational publisher, Pearson Scott Foresman is honored to reissue these classic Dick and Jane stories, with Grosset & Dunlap, a division of Penguin Young Readers Group. Reading has always been at the heart of everything we do, and we sincerely hope that reading is an important part of your life too.

Library of Congress Cataloging-in-Publication Data

Something funny.
       p. cm. — (Read with Dick and Jane ; 2)
Summary: A collection of reissued stories with simple vocabulary featuring Dick, Jane, and other familiar characters.
  ISBN 0-448-43401-6 (pbk.) — ISBN 0-448-43413-X (hardcover)
  1. Readers (Primary) [1. Readers.] I. Series.
  PE1119.S6728 2003
  428.6—dc22   2003016955

ISBN 0-448-43401-6 (pbk)   G H I J

ISBN 0-448-43413-X (GB)   B C D E F G H I J

Read with
Dick and Jane

Something Funny

GROSSET & DUNLAP • NEW YORK

Table of Contents

Dick

Look, Dick.

Look, look.

Oh, oh.
Look, Dick.

Oh, oh.

See, Dick.

Oh, see Dick.

Sally

Look, Sally.

Look, look.

See Jane.

Oh, Jane.

See Sally.

See little Sally.

Little, little Sally.

Look, Jane.

See funny Sally.

Oh, oh, oh.

Funny, little Sally.

Help, Help

Look, Dick.

See Spot.

Oh, see Spot.

Help, help.

Oh, Jane.

See Spot.

Oh, see Spot.

Come, Jane, come.

Help, help, help.

Look Dick.

See Spot and Sally.

Come see Sally.

See funny, little Sally.

Sally Sees Something

Come, Sally.
Come and look.
Come and see Sally.
Funny, little Sally.

Dick, Dick.

Help, help.

I see something.

Help, help, help.

I see something.

Look, Sally.

I see something.

I see Baby Sally.

Little Baby Sally.

Look, look.

See funny Baby Sally.

Something Funny

Look, Dick.
Look, look.
I see something funny.
Come and see.
Come and see Spot.

Oh, Jane.

I see something funny.

Come, Jane, come.

See Spot and Baby Sally.

Come and help.

Look Dick.

See Jane help Spot.

Oh, see something funny.

See little Spot.

Funny little Spot.

Make Something Funny

Oh, Dick, look.

I can make Tim and Puff.

Tim is yellow.

Puff is red.

Make something, Dick

Make something yellow.

Make something blue.

I can make something blue.

I can make blue cars.

I can make blue boats.

See my cars and boats.

See the funny blue boat.

See the funny blue car.

Look, Jane, look.

Up go the boats.

Up go the cars.

Up, up, go Tim and Puff.

Down come the boats.
Down come the cars.
Down comes Tim.
Down comes Puff.
Down,
        down,
                down.